This book is dedicated to our Lord and Savior, Jesus Christ. May His Resurrection Glory touch the hearts of those who read these pages with understanding, and may they experience His Resurrection Promise.

ZONDERKIDZ

A Royal Easter Story

Copyright © 2015 by Jeanna Young and Jacqueline Johnson
Illustrations © 2015 by Omar Aranda

Requests for information should be addressed to:

Zonderkidz, 3900 *Sparks Dr. SE*,
Grand Rapids, Michigan 49546

ISBN 978-0-310-74870-0

Editor: Mary Hassinger
Art direction & design: Michelle Lenger

Printed in China

15 16 17 18 19 / DHC / 22 21 20 19 18 17 16 15 14 13 12 11 10 9 8 7 6 5 4 3 2 1

A Royal Easter Story

WRITTEN BY **Jeanna Young** & **Jacqueline Johnson**

ILLUSTRATED BY **Omar Aranda**

Once upon a time, in a magnificent castle perched high on a hill, lived five princesses. Their names were Joy, Grace, Faith, Charity, and Hope. They were blessed to be the daughters of the King.

The eager princess sisters had waited all winter for warmer days and finally they were having the most spectacular spring in history! The kingdom was alive with resurrected beauty. Easter was only days away. The princesses' garden had flourished again and all their furry friends were caring for new life. The girls were enthusiastically singing and dancing in anticipation of the annual Easter Jubilee.

One sunny morning, the princesses were surprised to see riders approaching. A father and his noble sons waved as they fearlessly entered the castle gates.

"Hello," a young knight called out. "We are your new neighbors."

The sisters smiled as the group came closer.

They recognized the father as a newly instated knight of their father's round table. "Princesses, these are my sons, Timothy, Andrew, Jonathan, Christian, and Alexander," he said. "We are at the king's service."

"Thank you for coming," the king said as he joined his daughters. He had heard the horses too. "There is much to do, friends, to get ready for the kingdom's Easter celebration!"

At their father's gentle reminder, the princesses turned to go, calling, "We are pleased to meet you!" They had much to do as well.

"Girls, we still have so much to get ready!" Princess Hope sounded a little worried.

"I know. I can't wait until we start loading the wagons," Princess Grace replied.

"Daddy, may I ASK you a question? Why do we travel on a pilgrimage each year for Easter?" Princess Charity, the youngest, inquired.

"Well, the day's journey is a tradition. Every year all the people of our kingdom and beyond join to celebrate the resurrection of our Lord," the King explained. "The annual celebration helps keep harmony and peace between the lands as we remember all that Jesus has done for us."

"And this year, it is our turn to bring the cross, gifts, and the decorations," Princess Joy added happily.

The day to leave had finally arrived. It was cloudy, but spirits were high. The wagons were packed, the princesses and the king all set to go. Filled with excitement, the gaily decorated wagons pulled forward through the main gates of the castle. Suddenly, there was a loud . . . CRACK!

"Father! Stop!" the princesses shouted as they jumped from their seats. An axle had snapped and a wheel had fallen off one of the large wagons. "We will have to load another wagon and follow you as quickly as we can," said Princess Hope.

The king looked ready to protest. "Don't worry, Father! We can take care of this. You must go on ahead," Princess Faith assured him.

Instantly Sir Timothy rushed up. "We are at your command, Sir. My brothers and I will stay back to help," he pledged.

The King reluctantly gave them permission to stay behind. And a few hours later, a new wagon was loaded and they were on their way again.

Along the journey, the caravan reached a fork in the road. "We are going this way!" Princess Hope informed the young knights.

"Our father always takes this turn. It's a short cut," said Princess Joy.

"But we're sure this lane is much faster!" twins, Christian and Andrew, countered.

"We'll see! You take that road and we will take this one," Princess Grace challenged.

"Yeah! Let's race to see who gets there first!" Sir Timothy chimed in.

"Deal!" they all said in unison.

As the princesses turned down one way and the knights turned down the other, neither group noticed the dark clouds forming in the east or the flashes of bright lightning in the sky.

"Faster, Faith!" Princess Joy encouraged after they'd been racing down the road a bit. "We must beat the boys!"

Princess Faith declared, "We have made good time, sisters!"

"I'm hungry!" Princess Charity suddenly blurted out. "Do we have time for tea?"

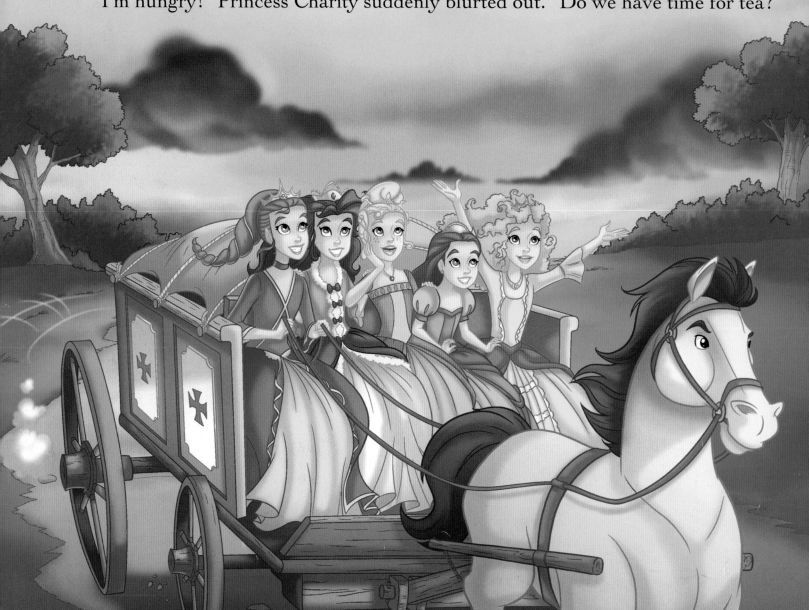

As the princesses took a break and swiftly sipped their tea and gobbled their cookies, a cherub-faced little girl silently peered at them through the trees surrounding their picnic spot.

Just then, loud thunder rolled overhead and Princess Joy noted, "Those dark clouds look very ominous."

"Yes. It's time to pack up. We need to … " started Princess Hope.

There was a quiet rustling in the trees.

"Wait!" Princess Joy interrupted. "Do you hear something?" She heard the rustling again.

"I do!" exclaimed Faith and Grace.

"Over there!" Charity pointed to the woods.

Running, the girls found the tiny girl who had been peeking at their tea party.

Hope scooped up the wee child and carried her back to the wagon.

"Sweet one, what is your name? Where is your mommy?" Grace asked.

"My name is Alina," the little maiden whispered. Wiping her cheeks, she told the princesses her story of getting separated from her family and being lost in the woods overnight.

"Can you help me find my way home?" Alina said with bright teary eyes as big as saucers.

"Of course! We will SEEK throughout the land to find your family," the girls answered.

As they wrapped Alina in a soft blanket and handed her a biscuit with strawberry jam, the first plump raindrops began to fall.

"I don't really care about winning the race anymore," Grace admitted.

"Me either!" Charity agreed.

"This must be what Daddy meant when he said to use our lives to help and care for others," recalled Hope.

"Not worrying about races and who's first," Faith chimed in.

Inspired, Grace stopped the wagon and gathered the girls together to pray. "Father God, you sent us on this path and we found our new little friend. Help us find our way in the rain. Give us wisdom to discover where Alina's family may be. Give us courage and guide our wagon. Amen."

Way ahead of the princesses, the young knights were overjoyed. They arrived first! It looked like they had triumphed over the girls. The king was grateful to see the young knights celebrating, but noticed there was only one wagon.

"Boys, where are my daughters?" the king asked.

"They should at least have reached the town walls by now," said Sir Jonathan worriedly. Andrew looked up at the king. "Sir, what should we do?"

"Send out a search party!" the king commanded.

The girls had ridden through terrible thunder, lightning, and a downpour of cold rain. It had gotten so dark it seemed like nighttime to the princesses as they rode on.

But finally, the storm ceased. The town walls rose in the distance beckoning the small group forward. They had found their way even in the storm! Sighing with relief, they rode through the welcoming gates up to the local nobleman's house. They raced to the entry and Charity KNOCKED. The king threw open the door to find his drenched daughters on the doorstep.

"Praise God you are safe!" the relieved father cried as he grabbed them all in one big hug. Then he noticed someone new.

Leaning down, the king peeked at the little bundle in Hope's arms. "Who is this?" he questioned, as he gently took hold of the sleepy little girl the princesses had rescued.

After warm baths and a hearty supper, everyone settled in front of the fire. Alina began to cry. "Mommy! I want my Mommy!"

Faith comforted her as best she could. "My Daddy and the devoted knights will find your mommy and bring her to us. Just wait and see."

This good news made the little girl finally smile.

Grace grabbed her own tiara and placed it on the small silky head. She burst out laughing with glee.

The sunrise was glorious that Easter morning. As the princesses and their father entered the Easter party gates, a frantic yet joyful-looking mother came running toward them.

"Mommy!" cried Alina, still wearing Grace's tiara. Mother and child seemed to fly across the lawn and into each other's arms.

The princesses clapped their hands with joy as the king declared, "Everyone who is lost can be found on Easter. Now … let the festivities begin!"

The annual Easter celebration began with a time of worship and honor for Jesus, the King of Kings. As families streamed to the outdoor festival, they were welcomed with music and stories of the first Easter. Later, a giant feast brought families from far and wide to celebrate in grand style. The gifts and decorations brought by the princesses and knights brightened the jubilee even more.

"To Him be the glory for He has risen!" the king declared.

And all the people said, "He has risen, indeed!"

Later, when they returned to the castle, the king beckoned his daughters to the parlor for a surprise. He gathered them near and said, "My daughters, I have a little something for each of you. I am so proud of you. You showed your loving hearts when you rescued Alina. You took such good care of her. Your concern for one of God's children was greater than winning a race!" Handing each one a basket filled with treats, the King lovingly affirmed each daughter by name.

"Oh, thank you, Daddy. They are beautiful!" the princesses said, gratefully.
The king smiled and replied, "My gifts are of this world. The best gifts come from heaven. The greatest is Jesus Himself."

Parable Thoughts

This story reminds us of one our Daddy reads to us from Luke 11:9–13. It is the teaching of a caring and selfless Good Father who not only gives us good gifts, but answers us when we seek Him. His life-lesson to a TRUE princess is that she must learn to lose her life serving others FIRST, no "I CAN BEAT YOU … ME FIRST." When racing the knights to the festival, we came upon a lost little girl who needed our help. We stopped our race against the boys, which we could have won, to give our attention to the more important needs of Alina. Her name means "light" and she opened our eyes to see the real race in life.

Easter is the celebration of our heavenly Father and King, who is "The Light". He is selfless and always focuses on others and the eternal … US! He gave the ultimate sacrifice—His life for ours on the cross! Not only did He die for us, but He is available to all children who ASK, SEEK, and KNOCK! This Easter, honor Jesus who died for you, by following His example. Go out with the message of good news— "Others first!" "So I say to you: Ask and it will be given to you; seek

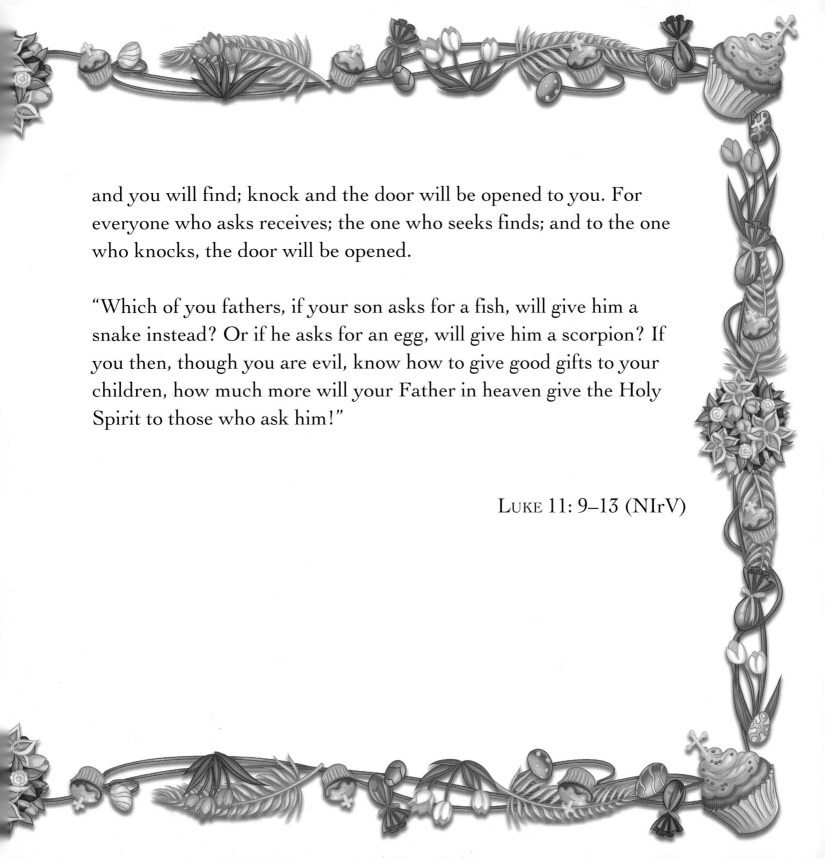

and you will find; knock and the door will be opened to you. For everyone who asks receives; the one who seeks finds; and to the one who knocks, the door will be opened.

"Which of you fathers, if your son asks for a fish, will give him a snake instead? Or if he asks for an egg, will give him a scorpion? If you then, though you are evil, know how to give good gifts to your children, how much more will your Father in heaven give the Holy Spirit to those who ask him!"

Luke 11: 9–13 (NIrV)